D0576024

The
Girls

For my girls, who made me the woman I am.
And especially for Siân, since we were "yea high." —L.A.

To all the strong women who have made me who I am.
And to my dad, who didn't get to see this book, but who always, always supported me. —J.L.

Sasha

Lottie

Alice

Leela

The Girls

Lauren Ace   Jenny Løvlie

RODALE
KiDS

Once there was a tree that grew apples . . .
and the friendship of little girls.

The four girls were as different as they were the same, and they were the best of friends.

There was Lottie, the adventurer, who was the first to find the tree.

Then there was Leela, who always had good ideas. It was Leela who decided that they should make the tree their Secret Meeting Place.

Sasha was the practical one.

When a very ambitious climber fell out of the tree, Sasha was the first one there to pick her up and dust her off.

And last, but by no means least, there was Alice, the performer, who had a talent for making everyone laugh.

Everything was more fun when the four girls were together.

Secrets, dreams, worries, and schemes; all were shared beneath the tree's branches.

Of course, there were times
when jokes went too far
and laughter turned to anger
and sometimes even tears.

But the girls all had kind hearts.
They knew how to say sorry
and learned something
from every falling-out.

The girls were very good at celebrating each other's successes . . .

. . . but even better at supporting each other . . .

. . . when things went wrong.

As the tree grew, the branches spread wider and the roots reached deeper into the ground.

Days passed when the busy girls didn't visit their tree at all.

Together and apart, the girls went on becoming who they were going to be.

They learned new things . . .

. . . shared new experiences . . .

. . . fell in love . . .

. . . and always took pride in their friendship.

As the girls grew, they remained rooted together.
When one heart was broken, they all felt the pain.

But they had built each other strong enough to heal.

The girls became women.

They worked hard.

They found new love.

They laid foundations for the future.

They had the world at their feet.

Leela continued to inspire them, and lots of other people, too.

Sasha was still looking after bruised apples.

Alice introduced a new friend to the group.

Adventures took Lottie far away, but she always brought her stories home.

The four women were still as different
as they were the same.

And they were still the best of friends.

Whatever the future might bring, if ever one of the women felt lost, they always knew where friendship could be found.